HOW A MOTHER WEANED HER GIRL FROM FAIRY TALES

ALSO BY KATE BERNHEIMER

FICTION

Office at Night (with Laird Hunt)

Horse, Flower, Bird

The Complete Tales of Lucy Gold

The Complete Tales of Merry Gold

The Complete Tales of Ketzia Gold

EDITED BOOKS

xo Orpheus: 50 New Myths

My Mother She Killed Me, My Father He Ate Me: Forty New Fairy Tales

Brothers and Beasts: An Anthology of Men on Fairy Tales

Mirror, Mirror on the Wall: Women Writers Explore Their Favorite Fairy Tales

CHILDREN'S BOOKS

The Girl in the Castle inside the Museum

The Girl Who Wouldn't Brush Her Hair

The Lonely Book

How a Mother Weaned Her Girl from Fairy Tales

Kate Bernheimer

COFFEE HOUSE PRESS
MINNEAPOLIS 2014

COVER + BOOK DESIGN by Linda Koutsky
INTERIOR ILLUSTRATIONS © Catherine Eyde
AUTHOR PHOTO © Cybele Knowles

Coffee House Press books are available to the trade through our primary distributor, Consortium Book Sales & Distribution, cbsd.com or (800) 283-3572. For personal orders, catalogs, or other information, write to: info@coffeehousepress.org.

Coffee House Press is a nonprofit literary publishing house. Support from private foundations, corporate giving programs, government programs, and generous individuals helps make the publication of our books possible. We gratefully acknowledge their support in detail in the back of this book.

To you and our many readers around the world,
we send our thanks for your continuing support.
Visit us at coffeehousepress.org.

LIBRARY OF CONGRESS CIP INFORMATION
Bernheimer, Kate.
[Short stories. Selections]
How a Mother Weaned Her Girl from Fairy Tales : Stories / by Kate Bernheimer.
pages cm
ISBN 978-1-56689-347-3 (Paperback)
ISBN 978-1-56689-348-0 (E-book)
I. Title.
PS3602.E76A6 2014
813'.6—dc23
2013035175

PRINTED IN THE UNITED STATES
FIRST EDITION | FIRST PRINTING

HOW A MOTHER WEANED HER GIRL FROM FAIRY TALES

For Mom

The fairy tale tells us
of the earliest arrangements
that mankind made
to shake off the nightmare
which the myth
had placed upon its chest.

—WALTER BENJAMIN

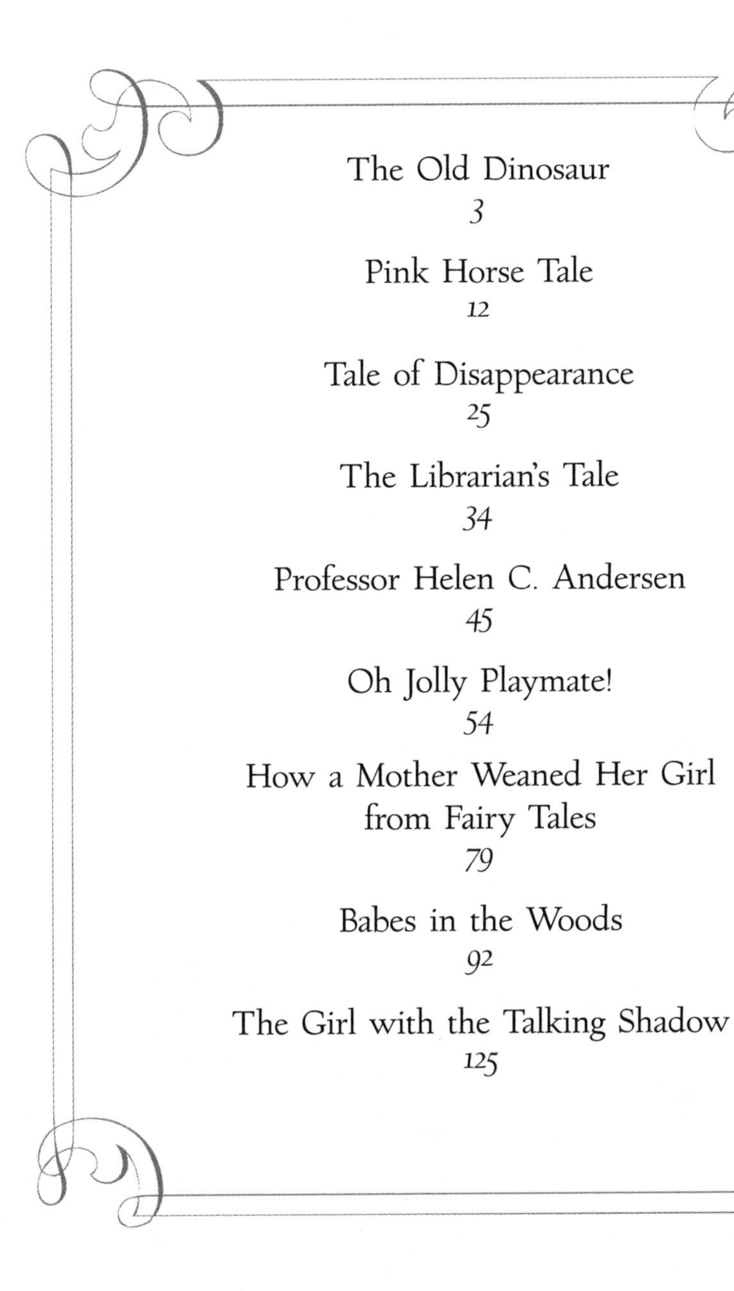

Girl from another planet, I'm yours. Your planet is small and difficult, but what planet isn't? I like your suit and your hands of metal flowers. I have always wanted a friend like you, you know. Also I can hear the vibrations come out of your helmet. That is the song I have always wanted to hear: the song of our friendship, and the song, also, of time. We will stay together here for a great while, I think—until someone finds us, I think. Girl from another planet, thank you for visiting us. It was unexpected, and nice.

The Old Dinosaur

An old dinosaur lived in a big city, and one evening he sat in his room all alone, thinking how he had first lost his wife, then his two children, then little by little all of his relatives, and then his last friend, a small child who had walked with him daily through the park blocks until that very evening. The old dinosaur was alone and forsaken. He was sad at heart—yes, that is the saying.

Hardest of all to bear, of course, was the loss of his two daughters, and the grieving for that never had ceased. Of course, as was reasonable, he blamed humans for his misfortunes. He was sitting quietly, deep in thought about this, when all at once he heard bells ringing from the white church down the street. He was surprised to find that he had stayed up all night in the armchair by the small fireplace. (Usually he climbed into bed in his giant pajamas on which were printed pandas and rainbows.)

The old dinosaur lit a lamp in the window. He left through the window, by flying. He was in no other way striking—he was pretty much an ordinary dinosaur guy.

When he arrived at the church it was lighted—a strange and diffuse glow filled the space. There were no candles burning. It was crowded, the pews overflowing. When the old dinosaur came to his usual row, it was occupied; so was the row in front of it; and so was the row in front of that one; and so on, and so on, to the front of the room. There, he turned around and stared at all of the humans who stood and stared back at him. They all held photographs: the photographs were of his relatives, the ones mentioned before, who had died.

The scene wasn't striking, but it had a strong feeling. The people were dressed in beautiful vintage clothing—the fabrics elegant, dusty, and dark. Their faces were pale. No one spoke and no one sang, yet the church was filled with a murmur—like bees, who also were gone from the planet. He thought of them then.

A woman—elderly, very stoop-shouldered—began to walk toward him slowly. As she got closer he saw that she was, in fact, a dinosaur too—and not only that, she was his beloved great aunt. She was dressed, now, in the manner of humans. She wore a black bonnet with lacy white trim. Her pale green dinosaur's face peeked out at him. In her hands, she held a photograph of herself torn out of a children's history book.

"Look at that altar," she said, taking his arm. "You will see your two daughters." And he did: he saw one hanging from gallows, the other tied to a wheel. "You see," said his great aunt. "That would have happened to them, if they had lived. The innocent children." Her eyes misted over. They stood there for a long time.

The old dinosaur flew home—this was difficult, as he was trembling—and as soon as he got through the window he kneeled on the hard, wooden floor. "I have seen mercy," he thought. He could not think of anything to do besides think about mercy. On the third day, he lay down and died.

He was the last dinosaur. My story is done.

Pink Horse Tale

A long time ago, I was very poor and often traded my body for cigarettes, Chelada, or food (these are listed in order of preference).

I had two children—both daughters—and together we lived in a motel on the coast. It was a knotty-pine kitchenette cabin, and had come furnished with a teapot, a few chipped flowered plates, some utensils, and bedding. The cabin overlooked a paved parking lot and beyond it, the beach.

If a man came to visit, I sent my youngest girl out to find driftwood and starfish and shells. (Her sister went to elementary school, so often was gone.) There was no market for these trinkets among the occasional tourists, but they were precious to my young girls, truly their only possessions. We carefully washed them and kept them along the edge of the porch rail outside, and on the white windowsills inside, which otherwise were totally bare, apart from a pink horse my youngest had found in the woods.

That pink horse, how she loved it.

Once, when she had gone a long way to gather her treasures—all the way through a natural tunnel that had grown inside the cliff, which led to a narrow beach that would trap you and kill you if you were stuck there during high tide—an old woman with pink hair approached her and sang her a song.

My daughter told me about this old woman. I almost didn't believe her. Later that week, the girl brought home a sea urchin, closed. She said that when the sea urchin opened, the old woman would return and on top of that, the old woman had promised to bring us good luck at that time.

I got an empty jar from the cupboard—a nice jar that had once been full of beach plum jelly but had long been gathering dust. My daughter and I walked down to the edge of the ocean and filled the jar with salt water. Back home, we placed the closed sea urchin carefully inside the jar. It quickly sunk, and stayed closed.

The next morning, my littlest girl didn't wake up.
The sea urchin had bloomed.

It was on her grave that my other daughter placed the pink horse. And then she too was taken—by the high tide—the very same week. She'd gone into the magic tunnel at a very bad time. Of course now I do nothing but drink Chelada all day, haunted by pink. Pink urchins, pink cigarettes. Pink horse, pink horse, pink horse on the grave—*if ever the pink horse flies into the sky, your daughters will come back to life.* The pink-haired old woman sang that to me once when I was passed out in the sand. For now, there you stand in the dark of the wood—beautiful, all-powerful, and silent.

Pink horse, you are everything, and everything is everlasting in you.

I'm yours. I will hold you to the sky until my arms get tired and then I will hold you some more. You are very serious. I understand that. It is nice how you gave me my outfit, the one with the knee socks and belt. Also I like to wear the slippers that match the stick handles when we go out. People might wonder why we do this—it is not the usual custom. But we so like to be together: you two gazing off into the distance, me loving you best. We will have each other for always: my legs and your sticks. We have serious eyes; some people think we have problems.

Tale of Disappearance

When I was still young, my sister told me there was a witch in the woods who tried to find little boys, and when she found them she ate them. My sister kept me safe from the witch, at least most of the time. Then my sister was taken. Before she was taken, she told me to disappear into the woods. She said this would save me.

She said, Brother, here are the things you'll need:

Cardboard
Brown Paint
Nails that Change Colors
Twigs, Six Inches Long, Half Inch Thick
Gold Bead
Large Fake Bird
Pruning Shears

Brother, she said. You may cut a piece of cardboard about five inches square, and you may paint it brown if desired, or if your chosen cardboard is not brown to begin with; this will help disguise the cardboard, which will then disguise you. Snip your twigs in half and glue them to the front of the cardboard. Keep doing this until you've made a small door with a handle. Then, take some more cardboard and make a good roof. And then glue a gold bead to the door's handle. Nip the legs from the fake bird with pruning shears. Make sure the top of each leg is flat and also is even. Cut a two-inch square of cardboard for each leg and glue these to the cut ends of the legs. Let the glue cure for ten minutes. Place the house on its back with the door facing up. Glue the bird's legs to the bottom. Let these cure for an hour before standing the house up onto the feet. The house should stand on its own—this is how you know a good house. Put the house in the woods and get inside of the house with all the nails. Hammer the nails into the cardboard. Then you are safe. If the witch sees you in there, she will think you're a witch. Also, the nails will change color along with the seasons and this will hide you from everyone else.

I did as she told me; I made the small house. This was one night, when the witch slept. Then I carried it carefully into the woods and set it down on the ground. I became small, I crawled inside, and then I hammered and hammered.

I'm still in here now, but it is cold and I am so lonely, even though crows visit the house and poke it with beaks. Sometimes they tip us right over—me and the house—and the nails stick in the ground and the fake bird legs poke up and only a hard wind will get us upright once again.

I don't really want to be found, but the problem with that is the complete solitude. When I had my sister, she told me great stories—now I only have fragments of those that I can even remember; I am very old now and do not have a good brain.

When I was still young, my sister would come from her bedroom in a pink nightgown and slippers—running into my room in the dark, with a flashlight. She'd perch on the edge of my bed with a big blue book of the witch's, the only book in the house, but she never read any words. She turned the pages and she recited, but I knew she said things the book itself never said, things about ukuleles and pirates and donkeys. She said, Brother, once upon a time there was a glittering and beautiful place full of pirates and donkeys and monkeys! Brother, once upon a time there was a land of card decks and sugar and saddles! The book's real words were not very good. I can't bear to say them; they were all very bad. Okay, I'll say one. It was *cock*—and the cock had a tail. It was *cocktail*. You know what I'm talking about.

So I don't read anymore, in my house made of nails. The paper would make too much noise and someone wicked might find me. Still, at least I'd have company then—did I mention that it's lonely in here? Did I tell you this house is too heavy for words?

The Librarian's Tale

As the town librarian, I don't have many opportunities for social contact—unless you count books. I live in a secret compartment behind the front desk: if you pull out the first volume of Louisa May Alcott's *Little Women* series, the entire wall swings completely wide open—and there's my apartment.

The apartment has just enough room for what one human might need: a wooden table with one wooden chair, a single mattress with a thin coverlet, and a one-burner stove. Teakettle, slippers, and candles.

I store all the food I need in the crate on the front stoop of the library, which used to be for returned books (no one comes to the library anymore, so I tuck my bread and cheese inside of the crate, wrapped in a kerchief). In summer I will leave a jar of water in there overnight; cools it off, which is nice. In the morning I sit on the stoop and sip from the jar as I watch the sun come up in the sky—it rises above the church across the road. (Behind the church is a hill that is good for moongazing.) When the sun is up, I take the skeleton key and pretend to use it to open the library door. This is in case anyone driving by happens to look: they will think that I am just then arriving to work.

No one knows that I sleep in the library—not even my mother, Professor Helen C. Andersen, who lives down the road. She thinks I live all the way over the hill toward the next town, in a small trailer she purchased for me and my sister and three elderly goats.

It is not that I don't like the trailer; I love it! It's a wonderful trailer: metal, with the sweetest casement windows you ever did see, and an awning with a picnic table underneath it. There's a tree swing under an elm near the barn. But when my sister died, I felt so sorry for those three elderly goats. They missed her a lot—she was the one who paid more attention to them.

It's not that I didn't love the goats, but they were so needy. I let them move into the trailer. They didn't take up much room, and it seemed that the company suited them well; they didn't yell at me as much as they had from the barn. They began to nibble at the curtains—who could blame them, as the pattern featured potatoes, carrots, and parsley—eventually I gave them the run of the place and moved into the bookcase apartment. I visit to freshen their water and give them some time out of doors on the lawn.

The thing is, I don't understand why no one ever comes to the library. Books are no different from goats! They enjoy an afternoon out on the lawn.

I try to rotate my attentions around—this is a small library, so each book gets a turn pretty often. Right now I am reading *The Goblin Market* by Christina Rossetti, which is a dark fairy tale featuring cats and rats in a very nice font. I have become a little catlike and ratlike—thinking, "Come buy, come buy" as I hear cars driving past. None of the drivers slow down; they seem not to notice the new blinking LIBRARY sign: I had expected that some might mistake it for a new bar.

My new desperation—I think it has to do with the weather. Winter is coming. And so it is good that behind the shelf, in my secret compartment, I have that woodstove. And I have all of the books one ever could need. Still, I worry about the goats and about my dead sister. I miss my good mother. I should visit all of them more.

I'm yours. I have some dark notions, but you glow green. You are cold to the touch and I like that. You make the light glow, except when it doesn't. That can be alarming, but I understand it is not your intention. My hand has no trouble holding you up—some might find that surprising or maybe they don't. They don't know how I feel—but who knows how anyone feels? Once upon a time, we found each other out here in the gray on mossy ground. That's something special. And you know what? I will share this with you. Since I have been yours my head is brimming with air and with trouble—or is it my body? It seems my soul has gone tired though my head has expanded. Still, I am yours and I will fill myself up with your spirit. It will bring us down to where I belong.

Professor Helen C. Andersen

The new fabulist moved into her office this week. It's next to my office. I asked my chair to assign her an office on the other end of the building, because I am a very private person, but he assigned her the office next to mine. My chair claims I will be a good mentor for her. He put in a one-way mirror between us so she could observe me. But why would I be a good mentor for her? She has streaky blonde hair with pale pink highlights; she wears three-inch heels and straight-legged jeans. Why would she need mentoring from me?

Let's be realistic. I have lived in this town for my entire forty-three years and wear my grandmother's clothes. I am not a good mentor for her. I can see that she judges my outfits by the way she watches me through her side of the mirror. My life was nice here, before. It was quiet. I did all my research at the town library, where my daughter is the librarian. There is a desk in the children's room always waiting for me. But then I was asked to keep watch over her.

She showed up in town with her pink-and-blonde hair and her new collection of stories about flying ponies, and everyone loved her on sight. I'm dutiful. I know my place. I started going to my office at school more often—in order to mentor her, of course. If I am asked to do something I do it. I am a realist that way.

And one must help the town's newest women fit in . . . it isn't easy for them. The women in this town can be . . . how to put this . . . so cold. My other daughter was a real victim of them.

How do you stay so thin, I asked the new one over lunch just today, in an effort to mentor her. Is it natural, or do you have a problem? I asked her. People in town may start to think you have a problem, I told her, if you do not gain weight.

As for me, I do have some problems. One of my problems is that when I sit down to write, I do not write about flying pink ponies. My stories do not come to me through telepathy, as the new fabulist says her stories come directly to her. "They appear on my forehead and I read them in the mirror," she told me, her eyes brimming with tears.

As for me, I have a very large forehead and it makes me look like a man. The more I drink, the more I become convinced this is so. I stare in the mirror a lot.

My new project is to find things out about her to expose the new fabulist as an imposter. For example, did you know she was once hospitalized for attempted suicide? I mean who does she think she is? One of my daughters? Or me? And pink ponies. Pink hair. This town was a lot nicer before her arrival, before she came here.

Now, when I look in the mirror, there is a terrible glare. She's on the other side of it—always—I fear.

Oh Jolly Playmate!

Pink Chiffon
Pink Lace
Pink Lady's Slippers
Pink Daisies
Pink Lace

We the undersigned will write all our poems on pink paper.

We the undersigned will write our poems on pink paper for now and forevermore.

We the undersigned promise to think pink.

We the undersigned forever pink.

We will wear pink every Saturday.

We will wear pink every Monday.

We will only write our poems on pink paper.

We the undersigned:

FOREVER PINK!

Once upon a time there were two girls. One had blonde hair, one had brown. The girl with blonde hair lived in a house made of stone. The girl with brown hair lived in a house made of wood. Both of the girls lived in houses surrounded by trees. Next to the wood house was a creek the girls called the Fake Creek. The water came from a pipe, rusted and buried into a hill. Across from the stone house flowed the Good Stream. The two girls had names for everything. Out by the Fake Creek and the Good Stream they would clasp hands and sing children's songs, though they were fourteen.

Oh jolly playmate,
Come out and play with me,
And bring your dollies three,
Climb up my apple tree,
Slide down my rainbow,
Into my cellar door,
And we'll be jolly friends,
Forevermore.

At the stone house, everything was brown and gray. Not just the stones: the light, and the walls. Sweaters the dark-haired mother wore. The wood house was brighter: pale green and overflowing with children. The blonde girl, named S—, envied the family that lived inside there. The brunette was named K— and she envied S—'s lonely fairy-tale cottage.

It was a real girlhood friendship. It was etched in the Book of Childhood Dreams. Yet with S—, K— felt herself growing older each day. This was unpleasant. The page was being turned before the picture could be colored in—there was a frantic feeling about this.

On hot summer evenings, the friends watched television in the attic of the stone house. The television perched on an old wooden table, its rabbit-ear antennae cocked to the side. In twilight they watched a show about supernatural things that happened in a strange, murky twilight. They planned it like this. The blonde girl's mother had forbidden the program from viewing, but the two girls really loved it. The show began with forbidding dark music . . . and the actors stared out of the screen. "This seems about evil," the blonde girl would comment. "It seems about evil," the brunette would agree.

Oh jolly playmate,
I cannot play with you.
My dolly has the flu,
The mumps and measles too.
I can't slide down your rain barrel,
And through your cellar door.
But we'll be jolly friends,
Forevermore, more, more, more, more.

On weekend afternoons they would ride on a green train to downtown and buy colorful earrings made of feathers—from peacocks and from other birds. Green, blue, black, and brown. And jackets made of green wool, dark green faded to gray—coats young men had maybe worn in the army, coats young men might have died in, they thought.

K—'s mother packed K— lunch every day in a brown paper bag. Even in summer (which it was when this story took place) she would pack a lunch for K— to take with her to S—'s house when she went over to play. Sandwiches wrapped in wax paper. S— and K— would split the sandwich on the green train when they were on their way downtown to buy feather earrings or the coats of dead men.

Up in the attic at S—'s house they were allowed only water, but they snuck food coloring into the room. "Drink me," they'd say to their glasses of water, dripping red in—they vowed to eat only pink food that summer. Summer of 1983.

On the train sometimes they'd plug cords into a yellow box that played music. Their friend P—, whose parents allowed her to drink vodka, had made them cassettes. They listened to these and also recorded songs of their own.

And her name is

P-I-N-K-Y

P-I-N, *no lie*

K-Y, *me-oh-my*

She's $69.95

Give her a try

P-I-N-K-Y

P-I-N *I cry*

K-Y *don't be shy*

$69.95, *boy*

Give her a try

It was a hot summer. It was once upon a time. It was the suburbs. They made themselves drinks to take into the woods and to the Good Stream. Silver thermos, crushed ice, and the reddest of wines.

Once upon a time, in that summer, the girls (one blonde-haired, one brown) wore pink skirts and pink checkered sneakers. They had recently seen an episode of *The Twilight Zone* in which a wife awoke from a dream and had forgotten her very own name. They replayed the scene near the Fake Creek. S— spread her arms to the sky. "I will now recite a poem about pink!" she exclaimed. Then she recited a long story-poem in which two girls (one blonde-haired, one brown) stood by a creek in pink clothes and invented a world in which no mothers went mad. S—'s mother had recently been forgetting to blow out the candles at night; this was on purpose. Fire trucks had to come on several occasions. On this day, the two friends walked back to the yellow wood house, where S— was also now living. The Apple Pie Family was home. They were treated to ice cream—it was white ice cream with Red Hots nested inside. As the treat melted, it turned into pink.

The girls fed each other. Pink dripped down their throats.

Say say my enemy,
Come out and fight with me,
And bring your weapons three,
Climb up my torture tree,
Slide down my razor blade,
Into my poison pit,
And we'll be jolly enemies,
Forevermore more,
Shut the door.

Once upon a time, in a town that was part of a city, two girls grew up who loved pink. They exchanged letters typed on pink paper (many years later, when e-letters were invented, they learned to turn the background of e-letters pink). They invented a dessert called the Pink Lady Slipper. At the market, they bought some ladyfingers. These were small cakes baked into the shape of large fingers. The girls filled them with Cool Whip swirled pink with red drops of dye. S— held a finger out to K—'s mouth, playing that K— was a witch and that she was Hansel.

Many years later, S— died. She thought no one had helped her and so she leapt from a window.

Think pink.

Drink pink.

The disaster is now.

I'm yours.
You do not know me.
You never will.

How a Mother Weaned Her Girl from Fairy Tales

There was once a mother whose only child loved fairy tales above all else and accepted as dolls only those that told stories. Of course, the child suffered as a result, for there were not many dolls that could perform such a task. Her mother suffered as well: when she went to the department store on birthdays or Christmas, she often left empty-handed, destined to disappoint her only child, who asked for more and more stories over the years. The child never said she was disappointed; she only said she wanted more fairy tales—that's all she ever wanted, she said. "The ones with the goriest endings. Find the dolls that can tell those, won't you please?"

By her fifteenth birthday the girl had precisely two dolls: one that told wonderful stories and one that told very bad stories. The girl was very good-natured. She told her mother, one cold winter evening, that even two dolls (one that could tell wonderful stories and one that could tell terrible stories) were better than no dolls, and that their household had more fairy tales than many far more impoverished homes, where perhaps no storytelling dolls had ever lived. And then she hugged her mother and kissed her good-night.

That very same night, at a late hour and after some vodka, the mother suddenly wondered—for the first time—how she might wean her daughter from fairy tales. Then there was a knock on the door. There stood a shivering doll—probably a witch, for she was life-sized—and she asked the mother for shelter. The girl's mother said, "Can you tell stories? My daughter does not allow any dolls in the house that cannot tell stories." The doll saw that she had no choice; she was a rag doll and she had gotten wet. She had icicles dangling off her yarn hair; her large fingers nearly were frozen, like links of meat one might keep in the freezer.

"I can."

"And will you tell them for a long time?"

"All night."

They agreed on some terms.

The mother let the doll in and set her in a rocking chair by the fire, where her cotton stuffing nicely and evenly warmed—but not too much. The mother gently woke up her daughter and said, "There is a doll here that has promised to tell stories all night, on the condition that your other dolls do not argue, or interrupt." The daughter woke up her dolls—the one that could tell good stories and the one that could tell bad stories—and brought them to the living room and sat near the hearth. The mother had laid out treats for them all (lollipops with chocolate centers in the miniature globes, jelly beans, toast).

The thawed doll spoke. "Yes, I will tell stories, but there must be no interruptions or I will tell no more stories to you." The mother, the daughter, and the two dolls ate their snacks and went back to their beds.

The doll began: "An owl flew by a garden, sat on a tree trunk, and drank some water. An owl flew by a garden, sat on a tree trunk, and drank some water. An owl flew by a garden, sat on a tree trunk, and drank some water." Over and over again, the doll repeated this sentence.

The good doll listened and said from her little doll bed, "That's a beautiful story, but I'm afraid your audience might become tired of it. I'm not tired of it, of course, I think it's a lovely story, but—"And then the bad doll shouted from *her* bed, "That's not even a story!"

The big doll gazed coldly into the fire. "Doll One, you've interrupted me. There were to be no interruptions. And Doll Two, you have interrupted and you have argued. That was only the beginning of the story. I was going to change it later. I was only just starting out." She stared at the fire. Her expression hardened—which was difficult as her whole head was made of a large walnut shell—and then the hardness turned into sadness. The big doll stood, and she sighed, and she picked up the two littler dolls from their beds. "I will take these with me and teach them how to behave." Then she flew out of a window.

The mother rushed to the daughter, who had been blissfully sleeping—dreaming the whole thing just like a character might in an old storybook: a frozen rag doll, walnut-headed and big, played the lead role in the dream, as if she were an old illustration drawn hovering above the girl's very head while she was sleeping. The mother knelt down, clasped the daughter's warm hands in her own, and said, "The dolls were *told* not to interrupt, and *never* to argue, and now look what's happened. They're both gone. You won't get any more fairy tales. They're trouble, I tell you, they're trouble."

The girl vowed never to ask for a talking doll ever again. Though smiling, she seemed very unhappy. The mother paced around the house for hours each day. "If only we had followed her rules—we could have seated the dolls in their miniature high chairs, taped over their little doll mouths, and listened to her fairy tales. Then we'd still have the dolls. We'd still have the fairy tales. We should have let her finish her story—it wasn't a very good story, but it was only beginning."

The daughter tried to comfort the mother. "At least we still have each other. Maybe she was just lonely—maybe she needed some friends. It was worse for her, really. She didn't know how to tell a good story." The daughter looked out the window at night, hoping to catch a glimpse of the dolls—it was something to hope for, anyway, that she might someday see them floating around in the dark sky, the big doll repeating her story over and over again while one small doll gently admonished, and the other berated, the tale.

"An owl flew by a garden, sat on a tree trunk, and drank some water. An owl flew by a garden, sat on a tree trunk, and drank some water. An owl flew by a garden, sat on a tree trunk, and drank some water . . ."

Babes in the Woods

One time there was a man with no wife and two daughters. Eventually he married a lovely woman he met in a bar. She was gentle and cool. She had a nice rock collection and enjoyed whittling slingshots, but she didn't like children. It wasn't that she disliked the girls specifically—it was children in general. Her dislike was more of a discomfort: children had so many needs and they were so vulnerable. It made her nervous and caused her to drink. She knew it would be better if she weren't a mother—for the children's sake, not for her own. She didn't want anyone to know about this; she was gentle and cool, and didn't like to hurt feelings.

Before she knew it, she began depriving the children of food. She knew this was wrong, but she thought maybe then they would leave on their own—find another home where they would be better fed and have a good mother. Or it could be they would prefer the starvation—you never knew, these days, sad as it was—and then maybe, as a result of their own unfortunate choosing, they would perish. She didn't really wish this, but she thought of it; that is, she got the idea or image, inside of her head.

The mother hid the cans of tomato soup first; the daughters loved tomato soup best. She did this furtively, for she knew it was wrong, but she still couldn't help it. Next she hid the sardines, which the children ate after school, on buttered slices of bread. She hid the potatoes; their eyes always bothered the elder girl, so these were not missed. She hid the apples, the cherries, the Slim Jims, the walnuts, the flour.

The father did not notice the missing items too quickly, because he did not frequent the pantry. At work every morning he bought an egg sandwich for breakfast, from a silver trailer outside of his office. At work he sold windowpanes—over the phone. Every evening he brought groceries home, but they always were gone by the morning. So it went like this for some weeks, until at last the children really were nearly starving to death.

One night, after two Jack and Gingers, the father wondered what he could do about the bad situation. The cupboards were barren; even the mice didn't visit. No matter how much food he brought home, still it all disappeared. "What kind of monster would do such a thing?" he asked the wife. "It doesn't make sense that He would allow our children to starve."

"He works in mysterious ways," his wife answered, pouring pink wine from a box. The wife slurred her words, adding, "We need to take the children where He can't harm them." She said, "Why not take the children away to the woods and slip off and leave them? Away from the monster." Surely, this would be better than their starving to death.

The father did not agree with the idea of leaving the children in nature, though he liked nature and often walked in the woods with the children, looking for birds. He told her she spoke nonsense, as she so often did, and he wished that she wouldn't. They argued. They drank. Then the mother quieted down, apologized, and comforted him. The comfort pleased both of them greatly and they found themselves in harmony, calm. They agreed she would seek some outside assistance for the whole situation.

So after the father left, refreshed and hopeful, for his work selling windowpanes, the children were called from bed to their mother's lap, and she held them in her long and beautiful arms; it seemed there were more than just two arms at that moment. To the younger daughter, it seemed there were eight arms. The eight-seeming arms offered great comfort to the children, and also to the young mother. It is strange how consolation may be sensed in many places, even places where things that are very bad happen. *The consolation of imaginary things is not imaginary,* as it is said.

The children gazed raptly upon their mother, whom they adored. She told them they were going on an adventure, and there wouldn't be time to change from their nightgowns. They were very weak and hardly could walk; but their mother had poached some eggs for them to eat as they set out. The younger sister didn't partake because she didn't like how eggs wiggled. "We're out here looking for fairy-tale monsters," the mother said to the girls as they walked on the pine needles. She was drunk.

"We like our ogres and witches," the girls said, holding her hands, one girl clinging hungrily to each side of her kind body.

"So you do, so you do," said their mother. "And your monsters as well." She tightened her hold on their warm little hands; never before had she been filled with such trepidation. She realized, slowly, it was the feeling of love: dread and fear for the children. This surprised her, because previously, she had not liked the children at all. Sometimes this sort of change simply happens in life. And so it was here. I won't do it, she thought. The conviction was total.

Yet, for some reason, when they were deep into the woods, she still went on with her plan. This is the way things happened for her—despite a decision to do one thing, she found herself doing another. Humans are foolish this way, which is a kind way of saying something about them. Brightly, the mother said they should go find some berries to eat. This would be old-fashioned, a real-life adventure. They were all so hungry, and they were the heroes of this very story: what a wonder it would be when they found berries and ate them and then they survived. That's how she got the girls away from her side. They loved their fairy-tale heroes as much as they loved their ogres and witches.

The mother ran home.

The girls wandered for weeks in the forest.

One day, they came upon a hut with the most wonderful sparkling windows, and they crept up and knocked on the door. An old witch came to the door and smiled at them; she said plainly, "Come in." They went in and told her their mother was trying to starve them to death and had left them in the woods in order that they might starve. "What a monster," this old witch, who was also a little witch, said. Unfortunately she also saw fit to settle them into a cage. The girls overheard her say to someone that they would soon be fat enough to kill, and then eat.

"Only a monster would harm little children," said someone who stepped into their view. This girl wore a white dress and a white bonnet and high, lace-up white boots. She had white hair and was smoking a rose-colored cigar, like the bubblegum kind they got in their Christmas stockings each year. She was the most beautiful person they ever had seen.

The witch snarled, "Don't speak to your mother that way. You are my only joy."

And so it went. For some months, maybe years, this young white-haired girl would tell them to stick their hands out so she could get a good feel of their fingers. That was the way her mother had asked her to measure whether they were fat and ready to eat. The elder girl would poke her large fingers out through the wires, but her sister would only hold out some sticks. The young witch would take a drag of her cigar and say to the older girl, "Gee, you're getting fat." But the sticks the younger sister stuck out felt hard and she would shudder and call her *skeletor,* fondly. Then she'd report to her mother that they weren't ready yet.

So it went on. Then, one evening, with no explanation, for none was necessary in a world where good and evil work in mysterious ways, the young witch took the older girl's hand and led her from the cage into the hut's cozy kitchen. With a shrug, she told the older sister to get in the oven. The older sister said simply, "I won't." The young witch shrugged again, and offered her a pale blue cigar. By now they were both teenagers, the older sister and the young witch. Together they sat by the oven, chatting a bit, passing the time companionably; they had become, in their way, really good friends.

Soon they heard the mother's footsteps. The older sister hid behind the oven, cupping both lit cigars inside of her palms. They got burned. "Mom, can you check on the fire?" the young witch said. The old witch opened the oven and the two girls rushed toward her, pushed her in, slammed the door shut, and ran like a pair of beautiful twins to let the little sister out of the cage.

And then they all ran toward the pale light that shone at the edge of the woods. They stopped by a tree now and then to have a smoke and a laugh.

They hadn't gone far before they ran into the father. He was looking for them as he had been doing nightly for years. When they saw him he was holding a flashlight in one hand and a pair of binoculars in the other and he was crying a bit. When he saw them, he began crying harder. He hugged them—not seeming to notice there were three girls, not only two—and he sat them down on some tree stumps.

He began to tell them a story. The father had arrived home from selling windowpanes one night, and he had seen his children were gone. He accused his wife of doing them harm. She had denied it—wept and drank gallons of wine. "I never would hurt them," she said. "I'm a good person." She was the one who called the police to report they were missing. The father and mother had held a press conference. "Dear Lord," she had wept for the cameras, "please return my dear girls to me."

A popular news show had covered the story. “The universe works in mysterious ways,” the blonde broadcaster said. “Pray for the girls in the woods, let us all pray. Also for soldiers.”

And then the mother went away—to a hospital—and the father was lonely. He had neither his daughters nor wife; he ate frozen dinners, not even thawing them out, after work every night. He listened to AM radio, and weeping he sang along. *If you could read my mind, love, what a tale my thoughts could tell*. Eventually the wife returned home. All was quiet and sad.

And then one day—the day we're discussing here, the day when the girls were running with the young witch through the woods—the father came upon them at last and told them this story.

The story's end was consoling. The father took them back home—the white-haired girl too, whom he loved right away as his own. Of course, the girls had undergone changes. They were chain-smokers—those pastel cigars, the ones that come over from England in all the colors of the rainbow, tidily arranged in a small box. The colors matched a series of rainbow fairy-tale books the girls had on their shelves, the books with the monsters and ogres and witches.

And how the three girls ruled the house—how they ruled! "To think of it," the father said. "To think I sold that witch her sparkling windows—and you three barely escaped."

The mother did everything she could to take care of their needs. Anything they wanted—books about vampires, skateboards, rainbow cigars—she provided to them. It was such a joy to do this that she often wept while doing the dishes, or while helping them with their homework.

The girls had a lot of schooling to catch up on; though they were gangly young women, they had been placed in fifth grade. At recess they hung out by the monkey bars, smoking. It was not the custom, but the school allowed this; the town was so grateful to have the children home safely they had changed some of the laws, including those about smoking (for minors who had been missing and found). Even the third girl, who hadn't disappeared into the woods, but who had only emerged out of the trees with no explanation, was considered quite special by all, as she should have been. All was well in the world.

By the light of a lamp in the shape of the earth, the mother read the same book every morning and night. It had no fairy stories inside it, but it did offer a path, and she never strayed from it again. And though she still wished to poison herself, only when she herself dies will that wish go away. And to this very day she is still living, you see. She lives for her daughters. That's the beauty of things.

Bird bird bird bird bird!
Bird bird bird bird bird!

Friend friend friend!
Friend friend friend!

I am yours to the end.

I am yours to the end.

The Girl with the Talking Shadow

My shadow learned to walk when I learned to walk, and her first word was also my own. When I lost my teeth, she lost her teeth too. The Tooth Fairy left me a quarter; my shadow left me her teeth—under my gums. Over time they grew in. My shadow was mean, but I always found her a comfort. Besides, there was no getting away from her, that much I knew. As fast as I'd run, she'd run. Wherever I'd go she went, bigger or smaller depending on the hour, but always there like a friend or a horror. And her gray aspect slid toward me from the ceiling at night—a mirror of me made of shadows—even when my eyes were closed I could see her. She had a vague edge, a definite darkness.

The older I grew the harsher she got—I don't think she liked the way my growing stretched her so thin. When I became a woman, I grew leagues not only in height but also in ethics. I thought of others before I thought of myself. Soon after that, the shadow girl began to trouble me badly. Her face held a constant and hideous smile. In the past, she had hardly broken even a tentative grin—just like me, whom my mother has always accused of having a grim demeanor.

Things got rough for a while, but we've worked everything out now, me and my shadow, me and that little dark curse of a being.

In the early days, it wasn't that bad.

The first day of preschool, in the red barn of Happy Acres, I was settling for a nap, ready to enter a spaced-out blissful condition on a sky-blue terrycloth mat to tinkling music beside a blonde girl wearing a pink-and-purple striped top with a zipper down its center and matching shorts. I thought she was the prettiest creature I ever had seen. So, like a monkey, I stretched out my lips and showed her my teeth; I'd learned to smile, of course! But the response I received was quite unexpected. The blonde girl in the purple-and-pink outfit made a horrid face when she saw me, and turned away. When I told my mother she said, "Don't be silly, it had nothing to do with you!" But that wasn't true. She saw my shadow, I'm sure.

The first day of kindergarten, we were asked to sit in a circle, to sing. I sat down next to Janie O'Malley. Her freckled face went white under her orange hair. She turned to me with her eyes burning bright, reached out, and pinched my hand. Her face was a white globe of meanness. I don't know if it was her face or her pinch that hurt me so much, but I do know I cried. "Go away," she hissed. "Why?" I asked. No answer.

We had to make rhymes later that year with our names. We'd just learned to read and to write. Oh, I was proud of my clever idea! Words, especially rhyming words, had quickly become my very good friends. "Cathy needs a bathy," I wrote very carefully, in crayon. I drew a claw-foot tub, white and gleaming. How I loved my nightly baths, a special time alone with my mother and with No More Tears. But everything went bad from there. Janie chased me home from school yelling, "Cathy needs a bathy! Cathy needs a bathy!"

That evening, when I looked in the mirror as I brushed my teeth before bed, my face simply burned and I could see it burning. I perched on the footstool into which my name was etched in red and blue and yellow letters—C A T H Y—and the happy, colorful letters became black and loomed in front of my eyes. Not like shadows, but like headstones.

And later that night, the shadow girl came to my room. She had been with me forever, since that very first day, but for the first time since then she told me her name. I woke up in the middle of the night, just as always. The moon shone into the room. I looked over to my sister's bed where she slept deeply. Meg-Anne's brown curls framed her face on the pillow. Even fast asleep she looked like the perfect creature she was; when awake she often played on her toy plastic guitar and sang over and over, "I am Meg-Anne!" Above her head, Wonder Woman curtains flapped in the wind; Wonder Woman was pointing her finger straight at me, a gleam in her eye. I noticed a movement on the ceiling; a shape on a string, dropping down.

Soon, on my night table, next to the music box with the twirling dancer inside, sat my shadow, my friend, glowing as the moon glows and as a star sparkles. With her legs crossed and in a puny green dress, just like my own green velvet dress, the one I had gotten at Grover Cronin's, she looked terribly sad. She cupped her hands over her mouth and whispered, "I'm Cathy." Then, she disappeared. I felt my heart beat hard, harder than ever before. She had levitated, hovered over my face. She flew not like a butterfly but more like a crow. And I noticed for the very first time that there were no wings on her back—only her shadow.

I told my best friend Lizzie about my shadow when we played the next afternoon. (Yes, I did have a friend for a time, but nothing lasts forever.) "Oooh!" she said. "Let's play that!" So with our two dolls, who were also best friends, we enacted the scene. It became our favorite game for several years to come. My doll played me and Lizzie's played Lizzie. We set the dolls up in their tiny toy beds. I'd put my hands over my mouth and whisper, "Cathy," and then I'd flap my hands together like they were a bird. Lizzie would sit the two dolls up in their beds and with her mouth make a big giant O! of surprise and fear.

Come to think of it, that's how Lizzie always looked at me: with surprise and fear.

In fourth grade, one of the last times we played the Shadow Game, we used my Polaroid to record it. "The camera is broken," Lizzie said dully, waiting for the photo to develop. The frame was filled with white light, nothing more. No sign of the dolls. Nothing but light, white and gleaming.

In fifth grade, the year I lost Lizzie's friendship, my class put on *Mary Poppins.* For the tea party scene, Mrs. O'Neill had rigged up a table and chairs to hang from the ceiling on ropes. All the girls wore party dresses in pink, blue, and green. Boys wore black suits with jackets and ties. We sang about candies and cakes. The table and chairs wobbled and danced. In the middle of the nonsense song about delicious foods, everything went black all of a sudden. When I opened my eyes I saw my shadow, dangling in a sparkling party dress from the ceiling. Like my dress, hers had ladybugs printed on it, and a clear plastic purse in the shape of a ladybug hung over her shoulder—dark circles under her eyes.

My shadow's shadow was a little bit broken.

Then everything went bright and I was arm in arm with Lizzie and Barbara, singing that song. Over my head, I saw the shadow girl, and out of the corner of my eye, I saw Lizzie also look up. She turned to me with terror . . . the dancing went on . . . and then I felt a sharp pinch on my behind. "I hate you, Cathy," Barbara said in my ear. She looked over my head at Lizzie. Lizzie glanced my way, then up at the ceiling (my shadow was gone). "I hate you too," Lizzie whispered. "I hate you, Cathy." Then there was a flash, my mother snapping her camera.

When my mother got the photo developed, in between Lizzie and Barbara, where I ought to be, is no one. A bright light, white and gleaming. "Damn it! I left you outside the frame," my mother said, when she saw it. For my mother those were very strong words. I believe now she was angry because she would have no proof later to show me how happy I was at one time. ("But you loved being in *Mary Poppins* with Lizzie!" she tells me sometimes.) Eventually, junior high came and things got much worse.

Still, sometimes, even after what I came to think of as the Poppins Episode, Lizzie would call me at home. Her voice was always very low on the phone, as if she was afraid someone would overhear her. But who? Her mother had always been so kind to me; she could hardly mind if Lizzie called. "How are you?" Lizzie would ask with concern. "I'm fine," I would answer, pretending not to be crying. I was always so happy she called! "Remember the Shadow Game?" I soon would ask, overcome with emotion, and things would go quiet on the other end of the line. "I have to go," she'd say then. Click went the phone. The day after, she would never say hi to me in school. She wouldn't look in my direction. I could not believe my good fortune when high school finally ended.

I stayed home, just as I always had wanted. Daily I walked to the library—I planned to work my way alphabetically through its circular rooms. But I especially wanted to read the books locked up in the cupboards in the Adult Room: those rainbow fairytale books! I always checked out as many as I could carry and then walked home through the woods. There, in the backyard, at a rotting picnic table, I would read. Around noon, I would go inside and make a peanut butter and jelly sandwich and wrap it in a blue bandana; I'd pour some water and drop some ice into an empty jelly jar. I'd carry the picnic out to the yard like a girl I'd read about in a children's book. For the very first time in my life since before the pink-and-purple shorts-suited girl at Happy Acres scowled at me, I experienced bliss.

At night, my shadow visited me. She'd drop from the ceiling in her tank top and undies—what I slept in too—and hover just over my pillow, her face close to mine. Into her ear, I'd whisper tales I had read. I told her about science, how the earth was heating up slowly. About novels, like the one about the girl whose half brother named Ram, "overtaken with lust," had impregnated her. Picture books—a baby chicken who lost its mother. "Are you my mother?" it asked a log.

Meg-Anne had already gone to college two years before, so my shadow and I had the bedroom all to ourselves. I'd fall asleep reading in bed—I'd covered Meg-Anne's bed with books, and sometimes I'd fall asleep lying on top of volumes and volumes—and then with a whoosh she'd appear. She was as big as I was then—five foot four—and had grown her hair long, just as I had. We both had hair past our shoulders: glorious shades of blonde, brown, and pink. We wore matching white undershirts, underwear embroidered with the days of the week, and both of us had the same necklace on: I had found two teeny dead frogs in the yard, and shellacked them, tying them onto a string. She could not believe I'd made her a present—her face lit up the room with a smile. She'd never smiled before, and the light that came from it was like sunrise, or sunset. I had begun to smoke cigarettes, a kind that came over the ocean in a pale blue box, with their name all in squiggles. They made me sick to my stomach, but I liked it. My girl smoked cigarettes too, as she dangled from the ceiling. We really had flowered!

Yet even though I had started to feel free—I mean not really free, but somewhat free, or at least left alone—my shadow seemed more severe as days went on. While I felt happier as summer progressed, she began to emit an intensity that I couldn't stand. Her eyes went mean . . . and she smoked more and more. She dropped from the ceiling fast, blowing smoke into my face. Still, somehow, her evening appearances remained a real comfort.

From time to time the shadow girl would tire of my tales, and read me stories out of books that she favored, but I'd shudder and ask her to stop. The stories she read me were from strange, tattered paperback novels and had titles like *Flower Children in Danger* and *Evil Horse-Loving Girls.* That I disliked the novels aggrieved her—I preferred happy stories of rainbows, flowers, and girls, and was particularly fond of a series of books about pegacorns, a rare species that is a cross between a unicorn and a Pegasus. I complained, because though I was shy, and self-hating, I was not timid on the subject of stories. Her flying went haywire when I complained.

All the while I continued to enjoy my trips to the library, and my new outfits and hair. I began to wear my grandmother's old clothes. I wore her fur stole, and petticoats. I read fairy book after fairy book. School ending for good was the best thing that ever had happened to me. Then, one night in August, my shadow appeared, and without a word dropped a box at my feet on the bed. I could tell my shadow was angry. I didn't touch the box, and she said nothing about it to me.

By the end of the summer, when I had wound my way around the library to Juvenile, having devoured Adult and Reference and the locked-up fairy-tale books, I started to take the long way home, not just through the small woods but into the forest. I walked down the path of pine needles.

One day, a boy I knew called down to me, from up in a tree. "I like your outfit," Plute said. Plute Peters, just a boy from Meg-Anne's class who worked at the gas station at Four Corners, about a mile away from the library and near the entrance to the woods. Plute. Plute! What a name. Who would name a kid something like that? I don't even know if it's short for anything. I was named Cathy, and that's usually short for Catherine, but it was all that I had been given. C-A-T-H-Y. P-L-U-T-E. Spelled aloud they sounded nice together, I thought. I had on a long white petticoat, under a ratty fur coat of my nana's. The coat had come with her all the way from Russia, on a boat, and it smelled like the sea, and like honey and roses. "Thank you," I answered, and began to walk faster. Books fell from my arms. Plute leaped down onto the ground, and then touched my shoulder. "What are you so scared of, Weinberg?" he said. "Nothing," I answered. And it was true.

"So sit down," he suggested, gesturing to a tree trunk. I sat on the tree trunk and folded my arms. I crossed my legs too, for good measure. I knew what happened to girls in the woods when they encountered man-strangers. Plute stood in front of me. "Excuse me," he said, with a blush. He always was strange, as much of a social reject at school as I had been. He disappeared behind the oak. Silence, and then I heard him peeing.

Then there was a giant shadow—something flapping in the air—a horrific sound. I leaped up and ran home. I looked over my shoulder, and saw Plute rushing out from behind the tree, zipping his fly. "Weinberg!" I heard him cry.

The next day, Plute was waiting for me on the tree trunk. In one hand, he held a bunch of fading hydrangea, and in the other, a little black leather notebook. He thrust both toward me. "These are for you, Weinberg," he said. I thanked him, took the flowers and notebook, and continued walking. I know this all sounds very mysterious and strange, but it wasn't. He was just a guy, and I was a girl. It was a nice sort of friendship, for rejects.

We met daily at the tree trunk after that, him on his break from the gas station and me on my way home to read. I'd smoke my foreign cigarettes and he'd compliment my outfits. He'd ask what I was reading and I'd show him my myth and fairy-tale books. He even liked me to read them to him. Seems he loved to be read to, just like a child. I didn't even notice that my shadow was gone. She'd been my only friend for so long; thinking back to those days in the woods, I can't quite wrap my brain around how I didn't notice her absence. And believe me, this is nothing symbolic—she just wasn't there. But he was. And after the first time we did it, there was a sound sort of like wind.

After that I could do nothing but sleep, and my head felt heavy and shrouded. Even when I was awake, it was like I was sleeping, or rather more like I was dreaming of sleep, aching for it. I had no thoughts of the library or the woods. All I wanted was sleep, and my mother. She was so kind—bringing me trays of food, quietly placing them on my night table with glasses of milk and some buttered toast. And then, one day as she set the tray down, I saw a tiny body scramble from beneath it. It hopped onto the floor, with lithe, quiet footsteps. Then it zipped up through the air like a bee, and flew into a crack in the ceiling.

When I next opened my eyes, the clock read midnight exactly. I turned on the lamp that my Aunt Sadie had left me when she died. The lamp has a round base that lights up like a moon. It gives off a comforting glow. Sometimes I turn it on and off just to watch the light happen. That night, my mother had left a tray of toast and alphabet soup. I reached for a piece of buttered white toast. I thought about how things had been getting better around the time I met Plute in the woods, but I was starting to feel funny again—exactly the way I'd felt at Happy Acres when the girl had said, "I hate you," and my shadow girl first appeared . . . I nibbled a corner of toast, and sipped some cold sugary tea, and drifted back to sleep with an old song in my head: "I won't grow up, don't want to go to school, won't learn the golden rule . . ."

When I woke up, my room was all in a haze. I squinted my eyes at all the familiar things: in one corner sat a model of a castle, with a water-filled moat that often leaked; on my desk was a long row of little dolls that were popular then. They came in glass jars; they had name cards attached to them with strings; they looked like teeny beauty queens. (I didn't much like them, now that I think about it.) On the shelves sat my collection of fairy tales from the library. I pulled the books down and pored over their pages. I was looking for a story about a baby in water, a water baby. "The Water Babies"? It reminded me of my dream, or my dream reminded me of the story . . .

But soon, I came across another tale I never had seen in all of my reading. It featured a girl who smiled at everything, but nothing ever smiled back. She was a quiet girl who buried her nose in books. Sometime after she "came into maturity" (as the storybooks often said), a boy did smile at her. She ran home to tell her father and he promptly sent her off to a bad fairy, who locked her in the basement without any books or heating. The bad fairy would slide plates of food under the door. Perhaps the food was magic; her clothes got smaller and smaller upon her, though the meals were meager. And something else: though it was freezing in the basement, she always was warm. One night, when she was so big her clothes had stretched right over her stomach (revealing it to look like a moon), a light—which I understood to be the bad fairy in the form of light—slid through a crack in the window, down the wall, and into the girl. And the next day, her clothes started to get bigger. And bigger. And bigger. Soon the bad fairy let her go home, where she was greeted with trumpets and dancing. But she never smiled again.

My mother brought me some supper. This time it was crackers and jelly, a tall glass of ginger ale. I ate a few bites. "Is the bad fairy on duty?" I asked. My mother gave me a strange and unpleasant glance, and left the room in a hurry. As I came out of the fog of deep sleep, my body began to have a bad feeling. The shadow girl, the sliver of light. Getting bigger, getting smaller again. A black box, and a coffin. I was covered in sweat. I fell back asleep, and woke much later again, still sweating. Above me hovered that box. It had wings jutting out of its edges. I batted my arms and heard a small whisper: "I won't grow up."

When I fell back asleep I had the most beautiful dream: me in a meadow, in a gilded storybook frame. Sitting there, I held out my hand. In my palm sat a tiny infant, gazing into my eyes. It stopped my breath—or I passed out or something, because when my mother came to fetch my dinner tray, I had gone pale—with a very slight blue tinge, just like when I was born. They took me to the hospital, and from there, to a halfway home for young girls in my condition.

Halfway. You're not home if you're only halfway there. I may have been stupid but I wasn't all the way stupid.

And then my boy came out too soon. On his birthday the sky was covered in clouds. No light to spread into a window and fill him with air. And now, I'm back home, in the house where I myself was a child. I spend all my time lying in bed. I listen to crows. I think of my boy. Up there, on the ceiling, I can see my own shadow.

Of course I find much consolation when my mother brings me a new fairy book from the library or a tray of food for my supper; last night, she made the most adorable pancakes that spelled C A T H Y. Tonight she has promised me alphabet soup—even to remove the letters I hated. Of course, my sister Meg-Anne complains that I'm freeloading. Poor girl just doesn't realize: nothing is ever free.

C

A

T

H

Y

That's me.

I'm yours. I am the girl with flowers for hands. It wasn't always this way but when I met you, I knew that I was yours, and so when I planted a garden I made sure to do it just right. It meant considering the angle of light. It meant taking things on—things you never intended. If things seem a bit gloomy, please don't be sorry. This is really a wonderful thing. Flowers are heavy, like boulders, when looked at just right. Because I am yours I am rosy—and trust me, I am quite strong. Everything dies: I'm not too young to know that particular story. I can hold the entire world up with my flowers. I love you. That is the beginning and end.

The End

Acknowledgments

Many thanks to all the magazines and books that have given homes to variations of these stories: *Booth Journal* ("The Librarian & Professor Helen C. Andersen"), *Endicott Studio* and *xo Orpheus: 50 New Myths* ("The Girl with the Talking Shadow"), *Monsters: An Anthology* and *The Flying Spaghetti Monster Anthology* ("Babes in the Woods"), *Ninth Letter* ("Tale of Disappearance"), *Puerto del Sol* ("Oh Jolly Playmate!"), *Significant Objects* ("Pink Horse Tale"), *Sonora Review* ("The Old Dinosaur"), and *The Story Prize* ("How a Mother Weaned Her Girl from Fairy Tales").

I would also like to acknowledge the source fairy tales for some of these stories: "The Old Man" (German), "The Rosebud" (German), "Baba Yaga" (Russian), *Peter Pan* by J. M. Barrie, "How a Husband Weaned His Wife from Fairy Tales" (Russian), and "Babes in the Woods" (Appalachian).

I also must thank the many family members, friends, colleagues, and beautiful students who have supported my fairy-tale habit over the years. I send extra gratitude for this book to Ander Monson, Ann Patchett (Patron Saint of Antibiotic Victims), Aurelie Sheehan, Catherine Eyde, Catriona McAra, Donald Haase, Jack Zipes, Joshua Marie Wilkinson, Joyelle McSweeney, Kathryn Davis, Laird Hunt, Lydia Millet, Maria Tatar, Rikki Ducornet and the Magical Intellectuals, Sabina Murray, Brian Oliu, Timothy Schaffert, and the Walker Art Center.

It is always a dream to work with everyone at Coffee House Press—real-life heroes to cherish.

Donna Tartt and Argosy Bookstore provided vital consolations as this book neared completion.

And finally, Brent Hendricks and Xia Bernheimer Hendricks (Angels, First Class): it's a wonderful life with you.

This book is in memory of a horse named Rudy—beloved family member of Willy and Lee—though he deserves a happier collection.

Funder Acknowledgments

Coffee House Press is an independent, nonprofit literary publisher. Our books are made possible through the generous support of grants and gifts from many foundations, corporate giving programs, state and federal support, and through donations from individuals who believe in the transformational power of literature. Coffee House Press receives major operating support from Amazon, the Bush Foundation, the Jerome Foundation, the McKnight Foundation, and from Target. This activity made possible by the voters of Minnesota through a Minnesota State Arts Board Operating Support grant, thanks to a legislative appropriation from the arts and cultural heritage fund, and a grant from the Wells Fargo Foundation Minnesota. Support for this title was received from the National Endowment for the Arts, a federal agency.

Coffee House also receives support from: several anonymous donors; Suzanne Allen; Elmer L. and Eleanor J. Andersen Foundation; Mary & David Anderson Family Foundation; Around Town Agency; Patricia Beithon; Bill Berkson; the E. Thomas Binger and Rebecca Rand Fund of the Minneapolis Foundation; the Patrick and Aimee Butler Family Foundation; the Buuck Family Foundation; Claire Casey; Jane Dalrymple-Hollo; Ruth Dayton; Stricker & Bruce Dayton; Dorsey & Whitney, LLP; Mary Ebert and Paul Stembler; Chris Fischbach and Katie Dublinski; Fredrikson & Byron, P.A.; Katharine

Freeman; Sally French; Jeffrey Hom; Carl and Heidi Horsch; Kenneth Kahn; Alex and Ada Katz; Stephen and Isabel Keating; the Kenneth Koch Literary Estate; Kathryn and Dean Koutsky; the Lenfestey Family Foundation; Carol and Aaron Mack; George Mack; Mary McDermid; Sjur Midness and Briar Andresen; the Nash Foundation; Peter and Jennifer Nelson; the Rehael Fund of the Minneapolis Foundation; Schwegman, Lundberg & Woessner, P.A; Kiki Smith; Jeffrey Sugerman and Sarah Schultz; Nan Swid; Patricia Tilton; the Archie D. & Bertha H. Walker Foundation; Stu Wilson and Mel Barker; the Woessner Freeman Family Foundation; Margaret and Angus Wurtele; and many other generous individual donors.

To you and our many readers across the country, we send our thanks for your continuing support.

Coffee House Press

The mission of Coffee House Press is to publish exciting, vital, and enduring authors of our time; to delight and inspire readers; to contribute to the cultural life of our community; and to enrich our literary heritage. By building on the best traditions of publishing and the book arts, we produce books that celebrate imagination, innovation in the craft of writing, and the many authentic voices of the American experience.

Visit us at coffeehousepress.org.

Colophon

How a Mother Weaned Her Girl from Fairy Tales was designed at Coffee House Press, in the historic Grain Belt Brewery's Bottling House near downtown Minneapolis. The text is set in Village Roman.

Kate recommends these Coffee House Press books

The Deep Zoo
Rikki Ducornet
Essays

Windeye
Brian Evenson
Stories

Kind One
Laird Hunt
A novel

A Girl is a Half-Formed Thing
Eimear McBride
A novel

Special Powers and Abilities
Raymond McDaniel
Poems

I Hotel
Karen Tei Yamashita
A novel

Kate Bernheimer has been called "one of the living masters of the fairy tale." She is the author of a novel trilogy and the story collections *Horse, Flower, Bird* and *How a Mother Weaned Her Girl from Fairy Tales,* and the editor of the World Fantasy Award–winning and best-selling *My Mother She Killed Me, My Father He Ate Me: Forty New Fairy Tales* and *xo Orpheus: Fifty New Myths*. She lives in Tucson, Arizona.